ABT

D0602118

7/96

COUNT
SILVERNOSE

A Story from Italy

retold by Eric A. Kimmel
illustrated by Omar Rayyan

Holiday House/New York

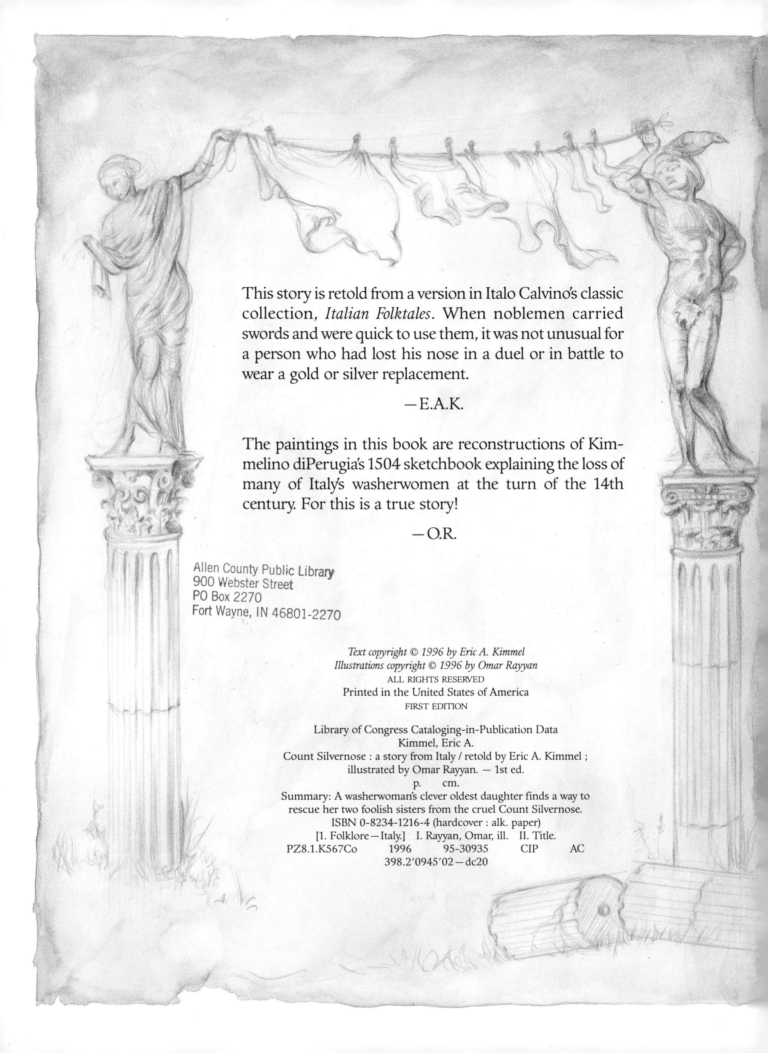

This story is retold from a version in Italo Calvino's classic collection, *Italian Folktales*. When noblemen carried swords and were quick to use them, it was not unusual for a person who had lost his nose in a duel or in battle to wear a gold or silver replacement.

—E.A.K.

The paintings in this book are reconstructions of Kimmelino diPerugia's 1504 sketchbook explaining the loss of many of Italy's washerwomen at the turn of the 14th century. For this is a true story!

—O.R.

Text copyright © 1996 by Eric A. Kimmel
Illustrations copyright © 1996 by Omar Rayyan
ALL RIGHTS RESERVED
Printed in the United States of America
FIRST EDITION

Library of Congress Cataloging-in-Publication Data
Kimmel, Eric A.
Count Silvernose : a story from Italy / retold by Eric A. Kimmel ;
illustrated by Omar Rayyan. — 1st ed.
p.   cm.
Summary: A washerwoman's clever oldest daughter finds a way to
rescue her two foolish sisters from the cruel Count Silvernose.
ISBN 0-8234-1216-4 (hardcover : alk. paper)
[1. Folklore—Italy.]   I. Rayyan, Omar, ill.   II. Title.
PZ8.1.K567Co   1996   95-30935   CIP   AC
398.2'0945'02—dc20

Once upon a time three sisters lived with their mother, an old washerwoman. The two youngest, Carmela and Maria, were empty-headed creatures with no more sense than a flock of sheep. They were forever prattling about fine clothes and handsome princes carrying them away to a castle where they would never have to scrub laundry again. The third sister, Assunta, knew that no prince would ever carry her off. She had broad shoulders and big feet. Her face was as ugly as a barn door. If that weren't enough, she had a wart on her nose and a glass eye. However, whatever Assunta lacked in beauty, she made up in cleverness. Above all, she loved her two foolish sisters and watched over them like a mother cat guards her kittens.

One day a gentleman on a black horse rode up to their door. The strangest thing about him was his nose, which was made of polished silver. He spoke to the old washerwoman.

"My name is Count Silvernose. I hear you have three daughters. I want one of them to be my servant."

"Take me! Take me!" Maria and Carmela fought to be the one to go. Maria pushed past her sister and leaped upon the count's horse. Off he rode. Assunta ran after them, shouting, "Foolish girl, come back! What do you know of this Silvernose? Where is he taking you? What will he do with you? No decent man wears a silver nose!"

But Maria, laughing, shut her ears to her sister's cries as she and Count Silvernose rode out of sight.

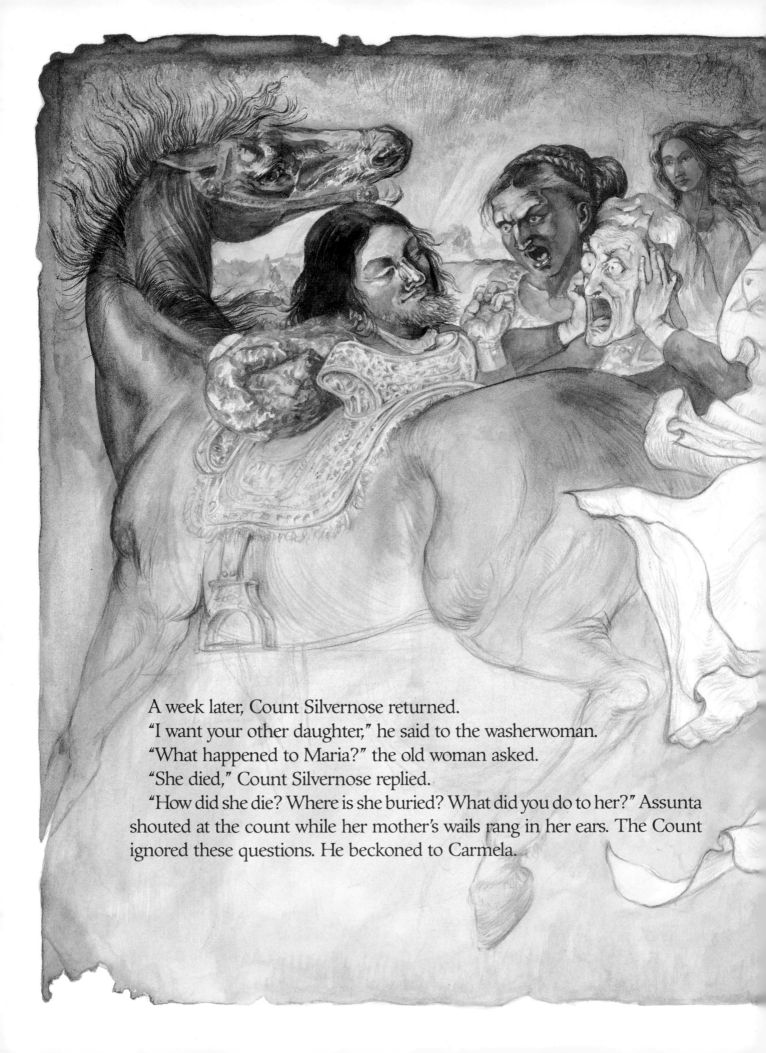

A week later, Count Silvernose returned.

"I want your other daughter," he said to the washerwoman.

"What happened to Maria?" the old woman asked.

"She died," Count Silvernose replied.

"How did she die? Where is she buried? What did you do to her?" Assunta shouted at the count while her mother's wails rang in her ears. The Count ignored these questions. He beckoned to Carmela.

"Come with me, Pretty One. You will have a new dress every day and hardly work at all."

Foolish Carmela, without another thought, mounted behind the stranger and rode away with him. Assunta, shouting and screaming, ran after her.

"Come back, Carmela! Don't trust him! Maria's fate will surely befall you!"

But Carmela turned her back on her sister. Soon she was out of sight.

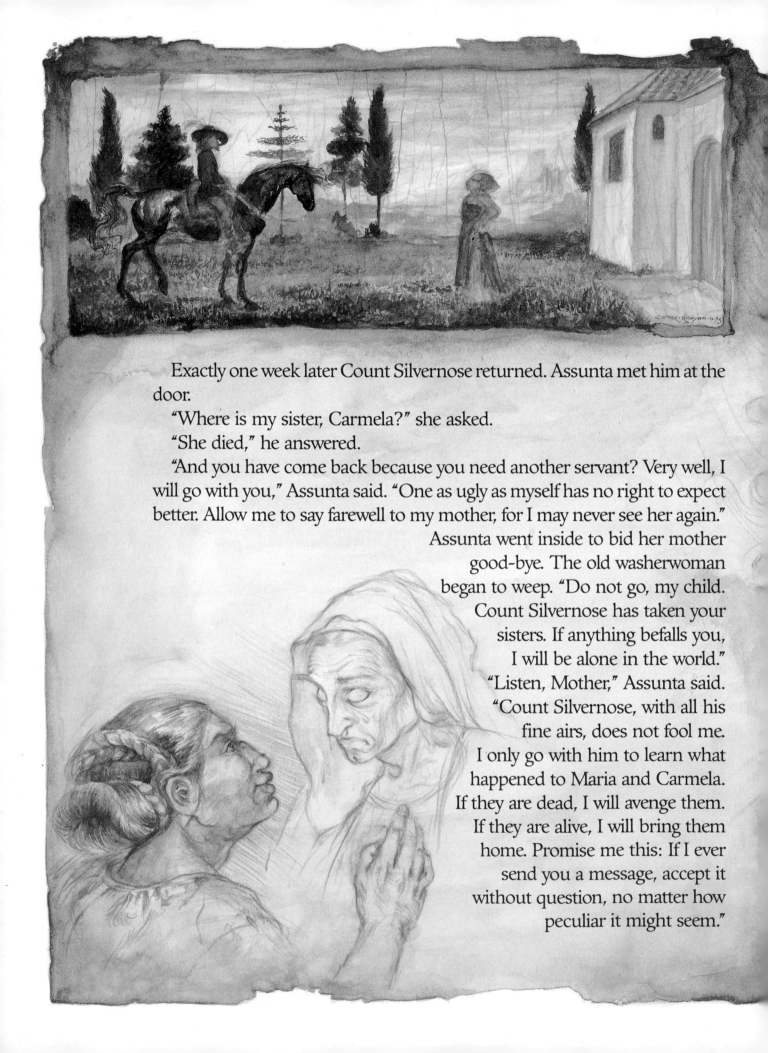

Exactly one week later Count Silvernose returned. Assunta met him at the door.

"Where is my sister, Carmela?" she asked.

"She died," he answered.

"And you have come back because you need another servant? Very well, I will go with you," Assunta said. "One as ugly as myself has no right to expect better. Allow me to say farewell to my mother, for I may never see her again."

Assunta went inside to bid her mother good-bye. The old washerwoman began to weep. "Do not go, my child. Count Silvernose has taken your sisters. If anything befalls you, I will be alone in the world."

"Listen, Mother," Assunta said. "Count Silvernose, with all his fine airs, does not fool me. I only go with him to learn what happened to Maria and Carmela. If they are dead, I will avenge them. If they are alive, I will bring them home. Promise me this: If I ever send you a message, accept it without question, no matter how peculiar it might seem."

Assunta's mother gave her promise. Assunta then kissed her good-bye, gathered up her few belongings, and mounted behind Count Silvernose on his tall black horse.

"Your sisters were not nearly as heavy as you," Count Silvernose exclaimed.

"I am built for hard work, not beauty," Assunta answered. "If you want me as your servant, you must take me as I am."

Count Silvernose grunted with displeasure, though he said nothing more. He spurred his horse, and off they rode.

They rode all that day and the next. On the morning of the third day they came to a tumbledown castle. "This is my home," Count Silvernose said.

Assunta peered inside. She saw thirteen doors that opened onto a long hallway. There was no furniture at all, except for a washtub and a washing paddle. Cobwebs hung from the walls. The whole castle looked as if it had not been swept in a hundred years.

"Come with me," Count Silvernose said. He took a ring of iron keys from a hook on the wall. He led Assunta down the hall, unlocking each door.

The first room was filled from floor to ceiling with dirty stockings.

The second was filled with dirty shirts.

The third was filled with dirty towels.

And the fourth was filled with dirty underwear.

Each room was worse than the one before it. Finally they came to the thirteenth door. Count Silvernose showed Assunta the key, but he did not open it.

"Whatever lies behind that door is secret. You must never unlock it or try to look inside. If you do, it will cost you dearly."

Assunta shrugged. "If you don't want me to open the door, why show me the key? Who cares what lies behind it anyway? More dirty laundry!"

Count Silvernose handed her the key ring, saying, "I will leave you now. When I return, I expect to find all these clothes washed, ironed, and put away."

"Do you?" Assunta said. "Well, I will do my best. You have no right to expect more."

Count Silvernose mounted his horse and rode away.
As soon as he was out of sight, Assunta took the
thirteenth key and fitted it into the lock on the door.

It opened.

Assunta stepped back in surprise.

Behind the door she found a smoking pit
of fire and brimstone. Her sisters lay at the
bottom, weeping in despair, tormented
by a host of imps and goblins.

"Maria! Carmela! Fear not!
I have come to rescue you!"
Assunta called down to them.

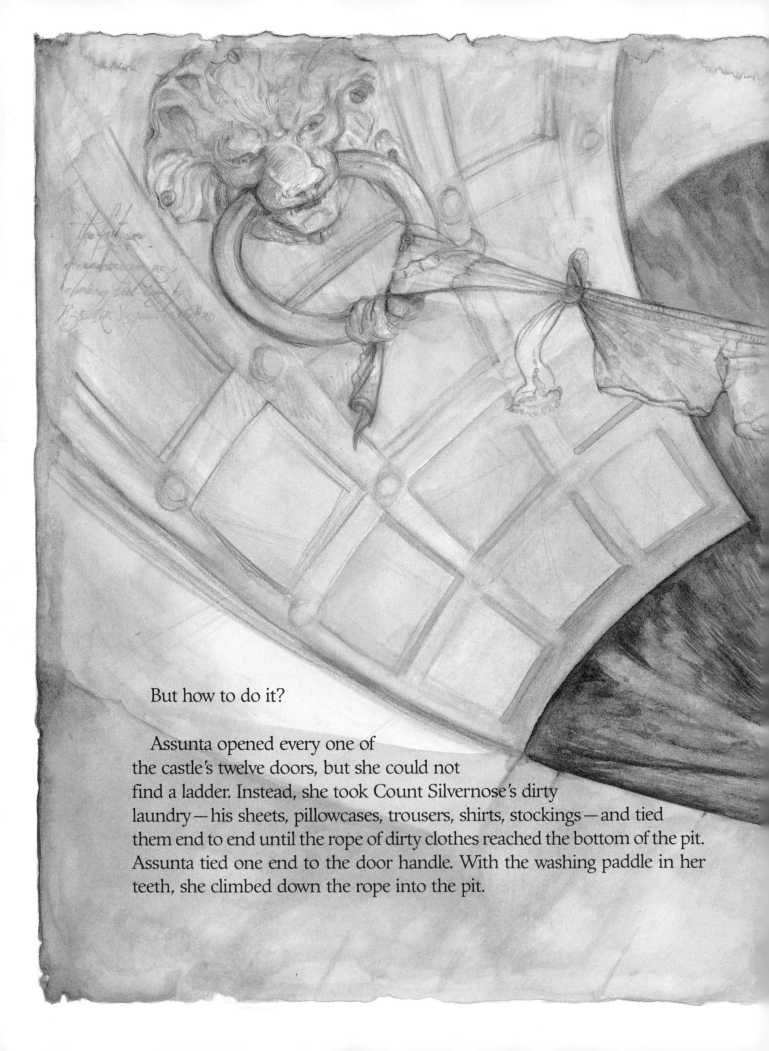

But how to do it?

Assunta opened every one of
the castle's twelve doors, but she could not
find a ladder. Instead, she took Count Silvernose's dirty
laundry—his sheets, pillowcases, trousers, shirts, stockings—and tied
them end to end until the rope of dirty clothes reached the bottom of the pit.
Assunta tied one end to the door handle. With the washing paddle in her
teeth, she climbed down the rope into the pit.

The imps and goblins attacked her savagely when she reached the bottom. But Assunta wielded the washing paddle with such vigor that she beat them all senseless.

"Maria, put your arms around my neck! Carmela, hold me around the waist." With her two sisters clinging to her tightly, Assunta climbed out of the pit.

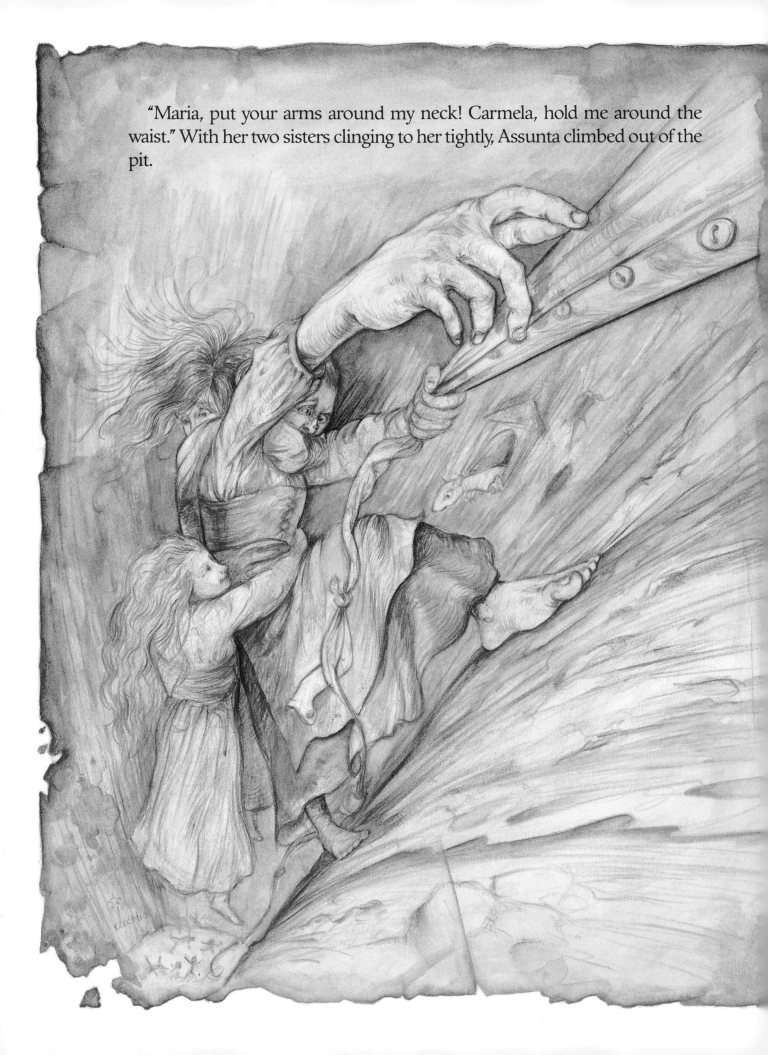

When they reached the top, the three sisters fell into each other's arms, weeping with joy.

"Count Silvernose will pay for what he has done to you. I smashed those goblins," Assunta said.

"Beware, Assunta! He is a dreadful hobgoblin, terribly strong and frightfully sly," Maria and Carmela warned her. "When we arrived at the castle, Count Silvernose showed us the twelve rooms. He gave us the key to the thirteenth, but told us never to open it. We promised not to, but when he went away, our curiosity got the better of us. We opened the thirteenth door and looked into that frightful pit. We thought Count Silvernose would never know, but when he returned, he smelled the scent of brimstone in our hair and knew that we had disobeyed him. He whipped us mercilessly, then dragged us to the pit and threw us in, saying he would wait until he had all three sisters. And then . . ." Maria and Carmela burst into tears. "We cannot go on. It is too terrible to describe. Ay, Assunta! Why didn't we listen to you? We will never be so foolish again."

"I am glad to hear that," Assunta said. "Much remains to be done. Count Silvernose will return soon. I must wash my hair to get the smell of brimstone out of it. Then I must think of a way to get you both out of his clutches so I can deal with him alone."

Assunta filled the washtub with hot water. With her sisters' help, she washed and dried her hair. Then she took a laundry hamper from the twelfth room. Maria and Carmela climbed inside. Assunta covered them with the Count's ruffled shirts. Taking out her glass eye, she placed it in the hamper too.

She said to her sisters, "Don't make a sound—unless Count Silvernose tries to look inside the hamper. Then you must cry out, as loud as you can, 'I see you! I see you!'"

Assunta closed the hamper. She tied a kerchief around her hair to protect it
from the smell of brimstone. Then she went through the castle, gathering all
the laundry that lay in the twelve rooms, and threw it into the fiery pit. Last,
she tossed the kerchief in too. Once that was done, she shut the thirteenth
door and locked it.

Soon afterward,
Count Silvernose returned to the castle.
He was pleased to find all twelve rooms empty of laundry.
"You didn't disobey me and look behind the thirteenth door, did you?"
he asked Assunta.

"Of course not!" Assunta said.

"Let me smell your hair."

Assunta bent down and let him smell her hair.

"It is damp. Did you wash it?" Count Silvernose said.

"Of course not!" Assunta replied. "When did I have time to wash my hair?
It is damp because I spent all day scrubbing your dirty laundry."

"And is it done?" Count Silvernose asked.

"Every bit of it," Assunta answered. "Except for your ruffled shirts. They have to be ironed a special way. I don't have the knack, but my mother does. I put them in the hamper. Take them to my mother's house. She will wash and iron them for you."

"I will do it now," Count Silvernose said. He lifted the hamper.

"Ugh! Why is it so heavy?"

"You have a lot of shirts," Assunta told him. "I had to fold each one carefully to fit them all in. Promise you won't disarrange them. To make sure, I put my glass eye in the hamper. If you break your promise, I will see you."

Count Silvernose promised not to meddle with the hamper. He loaded it on his horse and galloped away.

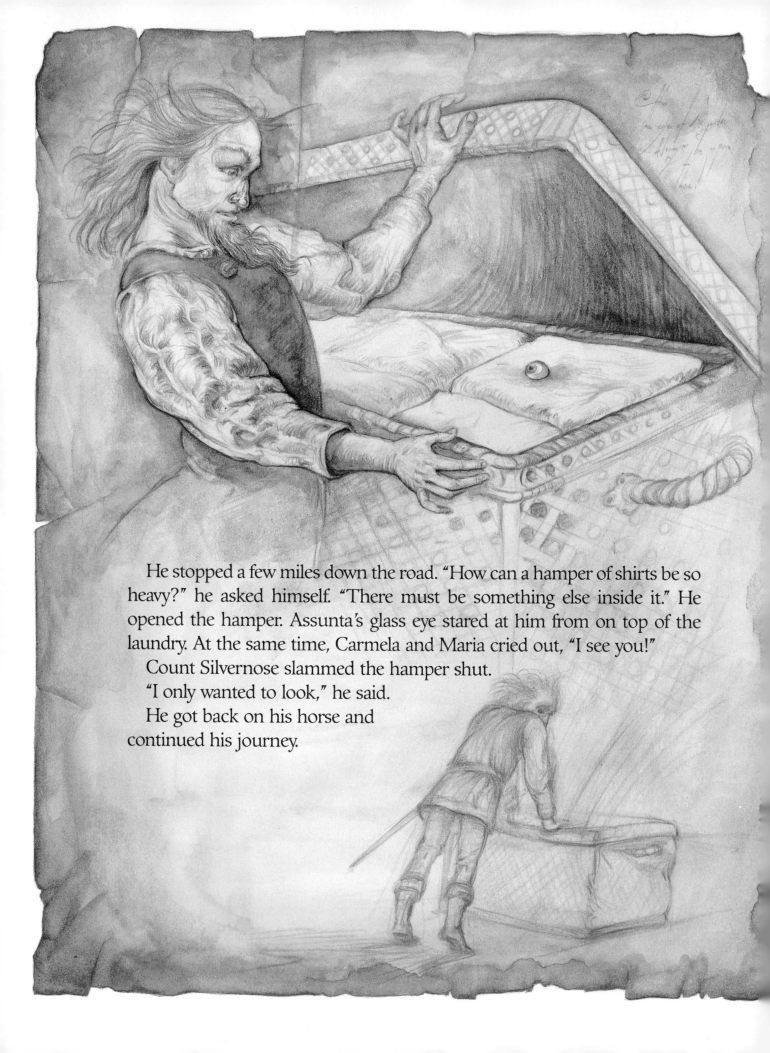

He stopped a few miles down the road. "How can a hamper of shirts be so heavy?" he asked himself. "There must be something else inside it." He opened the hamper. Assunta's glass eye stared at him from on top of the laundry. At the same time, Carmela and Maria cried out, "I see you!"

Count Silvernose slammed the hamper shut.

"I only wanted to look," he said.

He got back on his horse and continued his journey.

After a while he stopped a second time to give his horse a rest. "I am not going to open the hamper this time," he said aloud. "I only want to see what's in it." He pressed his face against the wickerwork. He saw the glass eye looking back at him. "I see you! I see you!" Maria and Carmela said again.

Unnerved, Count Silvernose got on his horse and rode without stopping until he reached the old washerwoman's home. He dropped the laundry hamper by her door.

"Assunta sends you these ruffled shirts. She says you can iron them better than she can."

Assunta's mother knew that Assunta was perfectly capable of ironing those shirts herself. However, she remembered her promise and asked no questions.

"They will be ready in three days," she told Count Silvernose.

"I will come back." The Count turned his horse and rode away.

Assunta's mother opened the hamper as soon as he was out of sight. She screamed when she found Assunta's glass eye resting on top. She screamed even louder when Maria and Carmela popped up and threw their arms around her. All three wept for joy, then for sorrow.

What would become of Assunta? How would she escape from Count Silvernose's clutches?

But Assunta already had a plan.

"You are a good girl. You work hard and you are obedient," Count Silvernose told Assunta when he returned to the castle. "I am going to show you something special. Come with me."

Assunta followed the count down the hallway. He stopped in front of the thirteenth door. "Open the lock," he said to Assunta.

"I'm not falling for your tricks," Assunta said. "If you want to unlock that door, do it yourself." She tossed him the ring of keys.

Count Silvernose placed the key in the lock and turned it. "Open the door," he told Assunta.

"Not me," Assunta said. "If you want to open that door, do it yourself."

Count Silvernose opened the door just wide enough to look inside. "Why are you so disagreeable?" he said to Assunta. "There is something wonderful in here that I want to share with you."

"If you think that smelly pit is so wonderful, look again!" Assunta shoved Count Silvernose through the door and into the pit. With a frightful scream, he plunged into the smoking brimstone.

Assunta slammed the door shut. She twisted the key back and forth in the lock until it broke. Then, taking the ring of keys with her, she leaped on the count's black horse and galloped away. She didn't stop until she reached home, where her mother and sisters welcomed her with great joy.

No one ever saw Count Silvernose again.
Only a pile of stones remains of his castle.
But the ring of iron keys still hangs in the
Church of Santa Maria Maggiore,
where Assunta left it. Visitors who look
carefully will notice that the end of the
thirteenth key is broken off.

For this is a true story.